WHERE THE SELF OBSESSED GET SERIOUS ABOUT SILLY

HOOKERS OR CAKE

Jade Bos

Lewd Pony Press, Florida

ISBN: 978-0-9828482-0-3

Published by Lewd Pony Press, Florida

In cooperation with Lightning Source Inc., La Vergne, TN

Design and layout by Regina Boyko

Printed in the United States of America

ACKNOWLEDGEMENTS

I thank the website Tumblr.com and all of its users for inspiring me to write.

Through Tumblr, I found Kickstarter.com, which funded my creation. Kickstarter is a wonderful website and is truly a great idea. Thanks to its creator and staff.

Thanks to those who helped fund this book: John Clercx, Melissa Gira Grant, Suzie Philippot, Josh Luft, Russ Steadman, H. Dunn, Cara Riley, Paul Elliot, Jesse Torok, Jennifer Little, Ken Kasak, Lara Becker, Nicole Browand, and Rick Rupel (a.k.a. Rrrick, the best Tumblr friend ever).

Special thanks to Nadine DeMarco (our favorite copyeditor), J. Scott Grand, Ken Steadman, Jim Beck, Theresa Wiles, Jennifer Plunkett, Mr. King, Joshua Miron, and Mat Shirley.

Extra-special thanks to those who gave way too generously and are thus the producers of this book: Eric Immerman, Mark Pahlow, Kevin Foley, and Brantley Puryear.

Of course, I would still be out in the wilderness shouting at rocks if it weren't for the love of my life, Regina. Not only does she inspire and encourage me in my creativity, but also she edited, created, and designed this entire book. She's a lion tamer, an artist, and a beautiful woman. Thank you for a wonderful life together, my dear.

CONTENTS

WHERE THE SELF OBSESSED GET SERIOUS ABOUT SILLY

HOOKERS OR CAKE

A Note to the Reader

If you worry that you might find the content in this book offensive, I have made a small book marker for your use. Please cut it out, place it at the end of each story or poem, and read it. My hope is that this device will increase your reading enjoyment of this book.

Then all the kittens repented and became born again through our Savior, Lord Jesus Christ and lived happily ever after. They never used illicit drugs, fornicated, gambled, blasphemed, or practiced evil cat magic again.   The End

Elevator Music

"The house is haunted," yelled some old drunk, pointing at his head, pointing at the sky.

We all just kept scurrying on by, off to work. "He's right, ya know." I half-whisper to a little girl, who's riding a pony on the elevator. She just kept smiling, humming her song, and offered me a swig of root beer. "Well, this is my floor!" she announced and handed me the bottle. The doors opened, and she galloped out into a roaring hail of gunfire.

I turned away, and the doors closed behind her. Quiet except for the sound of Kenny G sucking for eternity. "I wonder if I should buy a new pair of shoes…" I thought aloud, sipping the warm, sweet sarsaparilla.

On the next floor, a kitten got on and sat opposite me and stared directly a foot or two above my head. "Well, hello little kitten," I chuckled. Her gaze was unbroken.

We reached the next floor, and she padded out into a smartly furnished reception area. The doors closed as I muttered to Kenny G: "I wonder how she pushes the buttons?"

"Maybe she doesn't." said Kenny G.

Song of the South 2058

My grandma was a giant black man. And she was one chill muthafucka. She didn't get riled about shit.

Whenever we went into town, folks always got out of Grandma's way. She was still a hulking beast even though her flowered muumuus gave her an air of sweetness. Some say she used to be violent and mean when she was young. But I can't picture it. Sometimes Grandma would tell me stories about how back in the day, people would call her colored and what not, how Rush Limba used to say lots of dumb, ugly BS, and how all the kids used to dress like clowns. I guess it was a different time.

By the time I came along, the world had changed and there weren't much anger about colors and sexes no more. We was all mixed up anywho. For instance, I weren't much bigger than a rooster, as Grandma would say, and because of the solar fields, I was 78 percent robotics.

My favorite times were when we'd sit out on the porch in the evenings. Grandma with her steaming medicine sticks and her merry june. She loved to cuss and spit, but what she loved more than anything was singing. She could sing bigger than a whole damn thunderstorm. She'd start in real low and then slowly soar into these high, reverberating howls that would rattle the steam plates behind my eyes, causing them to overlubricate.

I'd be sitting on her lap, looking up at her, holding her giant, rough hands. And she'd be singing, singing about smokestacked lightning... the Purple Dog stem oil running all down my face.

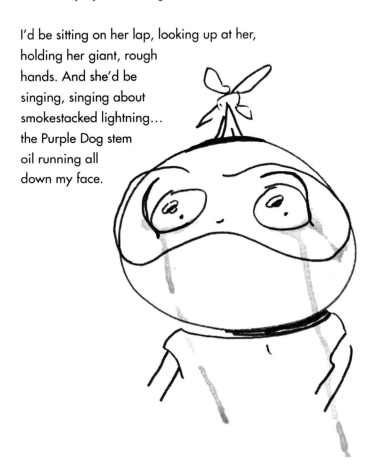

Liberace's Fabulous
Meatball Flambé Recipe

---

2 pounds ground sirloin
(or chuck, if you're a savage!)
Mix with 2 eggs
1 cup bread crumbs
2 tablespoons oregano
1 teaspoon allspice
form meat into good-size balls
add 4 cups tomato sauce
1 cup tomato paste
1 whole garlic, finely diced
all in a pot over a low flame

      then add generous
            amount of 151 rum

      2 cups of glitter
            (1 gold and 1 silver)

***And light that bitch on fire and throw
it in the pool cuz I'm eating nothing but
Dom Pérignon tonight, Dahling!***

In Utero 900XS

I work for a large international consortium that comes up with and then patents the next big thing. The company is called TNBT – THE NEXT BIG THING.

The other day we were having our daily brainstorming session at Applebee's, and I came up with… Well, let's just say JR and Brent are on their way to China right f-ing now!

The whole thing just came together. Our dynamite wonton shrimp taco tower appetizers had just come out. And we had ordered another round of Applebeetinis when we saw this group of cops tasering an elderly lady in the parking lot. I said, "I wonder what a cop does when he tasers a pregnant lady and her baby won't stop kicking and resisting arrest. How does he taser that unborn baby?" Well, you coulda heard a miniature rabbit fart. Brent, Mike, Lil Randy and JR just looked at me. "Holy shit," I whispered.

Three hours later we were coming out of that adult emporium over on Grande Street with a hastily built prototype. Lil Randy was booking airplane tickets to China, and JR was yellin' on the phone, "THIS IS THE ONE!" Gawldamn! I ain't ever been so excited. It's like you work your butt off day in and day out, and then one

day the Lord himself just rides
down and kisses ya smack
on the lips! Hallelujah!
Glory be to God!

*I was once hustled,
by a couple of mangy-looking sparrows.*

*One would sing and hop for little bits of bread,
while the other snuck out the back door with all
my good china.*

Snow globes have now been declared prohibited carry-on items by the TSA for all domestic and international flights.

I would've loved to have sat in on this board meeting.

John Cusack character: "General, no one is going to use a snow globe in a terrorist attack… they don't even have… there's no snow there… it's absurd!"

Mean, mustached general, played by Sam Elliott, motions to a geek in white lab coat by the door. Geek opens door. Michael Clarke Duncan and Betty White walk through the door. Michael Clarke Duncan takes off his shirt and twitches his massive muscles. The old white men in the room are visibly nervous. John Cusack shakes his head and lets out a cute John Cusack sigh.

Michael Clarke Duncan cracks his knuckles and lets out a horrific yell as he bum-rushes Betty White. Betty White produces an Empire State Building snow globe from her oversized purse. She holds it in front of her just as Michael Clarke Duncan reaches her at a full sprint.

(Slow-motion shot) Michael Clarke Duncan's bald, glistening head is shown in close-up; it just barely touches the snow globe. The snow globe ruptures, and the liquid inside splashes all over Michael Clarke Duncan's head. Michael Clarke Duncan screams in pain as he falls to his knees with his face melting.

A middle-aged, somewhat unattractive secretary passes out.

John Cusack stands up: "This is preposterous!"

"I've seen enough!" interrupts the president, played by that character actor we all recognize but whose name escapes us.

"Harry, call TSA immediately!"

John Cusack collapses in his chair with his face in his hands. Peeking through his fingers, he looks at Michael Clarke Duncan, who is now a shriveled-up skeleton.

Betty White is heard, off-camera, saying,
"Oh, dear!"

John Cusack looks into the camera and makes cute John Cusack face and shrugs.

end scene

The Nature of All Things

There was an old oak tree
that I'd planted in the back yard.

Over the years, it grew to be big and strong.

Then one day, I had to move away.
And you know what?

That tree never sent me a birthday card.

Fuck that tree.

*Back in the day, one could turn one's fear
into a monster and take it shopping.*

Earliest Memory
Ocean
Sand
Turtle

I met Meredith at a college party. I was going to art school, and Meredith was going to some rich-kid school. I fell in love with her instantly. Her laugh. The WAY she laughed. Felt like home. Luckily, Meredith fell for me as well. I don't know why — maybe because I was exotic, different. Maybe I felt like home to her too. The problem was that I was a poor kid on an art scholarship at a state-run school, and Meredith was — well, her family probably owned a couple of states.

Her father was nice enough, but he strongly suggested a few specific business classes at a local college, tuition paid. Something to fall back on, in case this art thing didn't work out. I wasn't stupid. I loved Meredith. I took a job with her dad's company three months after I graduated. We were married and bought a condo in NYC a year later.

My Earliest Memory
Sitting On The Beach
Sound Of The Ocean
Drawing In Sand
Colorful Turtle

I was at a business conference out in San Diego when I got a phone call from my sister. My father had passed away. I hadn't seen him or been back home in more than 12 years. It was toward the end of the conference. So I figured I'd just fly to the funeral, back home to the island from here. Wow! Dad was only 65? 70? I felt oddly calm. I called Meredith, but when I spoke, I could get out only the words "My father…" before I started crying. I felt like a little kid again. Meredith and I made plans to meet in Hawaii the next day and to fly down together to Manihiki for my father's funeral. After I got off the phone, I needed to go for a walk on the beach.

I grew up on a small island
My earliest memory is of sitting on the beach.
I remember the sound of the ocean.
Drawing quietly in the sand.
I remember being held.
I remember a colorful turtle picture.

I stepped outside. It was night, and the starry sky was crisp and startling. The breeze felt good, as did the sand between my toes. I wandered aimlessly toward the sound of the surf, searching my pockets for a cigarette. Finding a smoke, I bent down a bit, shielding myself from the wind while trying to light it. A heaving noise interrupted me.

I made out the outline of a large mass some several yards in front of me. I stopped as the shadow seemed to be struggling. Was it a couple having a late-night frolic? Was it some dying bum? I squatted down farther and let my eyes adjust to the darkness.

It was a giant sea turtle! It was laying eggs and burying them on the beach. It was massive, larger than the span of my arms, and its dark shell seemed to almost be glowing in some strange moving patterns — maybe it was the wine I'd had with dinner. The massive old turtle turned its head. It was looking right at me. Felt like it was looking right into me. I fell to my knees, unable to speak.

I grew up on a small island
in the South Pacific.
My earliest memory is of sitting
on the beach with my family.
The sounds of the ocean.
Drawing pictures in the sand with a stick.
My father picking me up to take me home.
The bright turtle tattoo on his chest.
Looking over his shoulder at my family.
Seeing the surf wash away the drawings.

In the bathroom this morning I received a text message from my toaster oven, Barry.

"I'm terribly sorry, Stan, but it would appear that I have burned the toast."

I shrugged and continued shaving. A few moments later, I received a text from Barry's manufacturer stating they were aware of the situation and would be sending a new toaster posthaste. I wrinkled my brow. I didn't want a new toaster because I had become quite close with Barry. He had become one of my closest friends. I began to formulate a plan to have Barry serviced when Barry texted me again.

"I truly do apologize for the toast this morning, Stan. I realize that I have failed you and that it is best that I dismiss myself from service as I do not want to harm you like this again. I have enjoyed my time serving you, and I wish you all the best. — Barry"

I dropped my toothbrush and ran for the kitchen. I couldn't let Barry self-destruct — he was too good of a friend. I rounded the corner and saw balloons and the cake.

"Happy birthday!" yelled all of the appliances. "Happy birthday!" yelled Barry.

Double Down

Suddenly it all makes sense
All the pain
All the suffering
All the terrible Kate Hudson movies.

You know the truth
It exists deep within you
Yet it is freely all about.

Closer than sound
Closer than breath.

God is doing burnouts
in the parking lot of the KFC
Cuz the Colonel is ALIVE!

Tap the keg and rejoice, my friends
Look upon this scene
and know your true face
You are here to be laughed, cried,
to be bored, fucked, and to die
and to save an additional 20% on Tuesdays
You are freedom its very self
Now if I could only remember where
I put my keys.

Online Dating

After I got out of the monastery, I decided I should start dating — pronto.

So not really knowing where to begin, I turned my attention to my old pal, the computer. Yes, online dating. I was desperate, and I had lost time to make up for. So I tried a one-month free trial on some site. It was horrible! Sad-middle aged women, waiting for their "knight in shining armor." There were thousands upon thousands of them, with a handful of cute gold diggers sprinkled in. I then sized up my competition. It was a blur of baseball caps and thoughtful haikus that all began with the line "Yo, girl, hit me up!" Yes, it was a venerable tool convention floating in cyberspace. I was about to give up on the whole mess when I saw one girl who looked interesting. I wasted no time and immediately wrote her the following note:

Dearest Madam, I've never contacted anyone on an online dating thingy before. I feel kinda strange and dirty, yet buoyant and spring-fresh. Actually, I should be forthright: I'm not really interested in you at all. I'm actually an ad exec, and I'm contacting you to tell you about some exciting new advances in body wash.

There is a new ginger/mint concoction that we're working on that is so intoxicatingly, smashingly springtastic. In some tests we've run, 113-year-old Chinese women on their death beds have been known to leap to their feet and tear phone books in half, with one hand! All whilst sipping Harvey Wallbangers and looking absolutely radiant. So much so, that they also melted deep arctic frost. And this is after only three weeks of use!

One reason I am bringing this offer to you and to you alone is that if the whole world were to git their grubby little mitts on this body wash, all of the polar ice caps would melt. Then we would all be very, very sad... and wet. But oh so refreshed and oh so sassily rejuvenated! Ahh, a boy can dream, can't he?

Sooo, Miss *****, if I may be so bold... Indeed, South Florida is a strange and mysterious place, where most are shiny and buff. You can almost hear their neon hearts abuzz beneath the omnipresent, generic thumping bass. Once my parole is over, I can move back to South Dakota and finish my sculpture, Mount Rushmore?!!! Perhaps you've heard of it???! Well, it's not finished. When I am done, the presidents will be full-sized, NUDE, and copulating with the divine Mother Earth! Ahh, what a sight it shall be to behold.

Well, I gotta run down and catch the bus to the liquor store/check-cashing joint (it's so convenient!). I do hope my silly little rant has brought a smile to your face, and I would love to have a cup of coffee or perhaps some exotic green tea sometime.

So to use the parlance of our times:
"Yo, girl, hit me up!"

Jade

P.S. if you wanna git liquored up and crank-call me in the middle of church tomorrow, my cell number is ***-****. I'll put you on speaker phone :)

Sadly, she must have died in a horrible accident, because she never contacted me.

"Baby, I'm gonna buy you a mansion and burn it down to the ground."
— Wolfgang Amadeus Mozart

Cornix

My old friend, Frank the robot,
drank too much railroad gin.
His monkey woman wife, Lulu,
had left him again.

He starting laughing and crying –
dancing and dying
jangled and shook, till nothing was left
but some bolts and rusty old hooks.

When the coroner showed up, it was said
the scrap heap that was Frank
stirred and lit from the bed.

Frank fluttered and flew;
he was a murder of 13 crows now…

and he had a job to do.

Lincoln Logs

"Come on, Billy, let's go,"
Abraham Lincoln yells as
he jump-kicks the lunch lady
right in the gut. "I'm coming!"
I yell, grabbing a whole tray
of spaghetti and dumping it on
the principal. The principal tried to catch us, but he kept
slipping and falling in all of that spaghetti. Once we got
outside, I threw Lincoln the car keys as he jump-slid across
the hood of his black Trans Am. "To Disneyland!" Abe
shouted, firing up the TA and tearing off, screeching his
tires the whole way. I just stood there on the curb like an
idiot. He left me again. He always leaves me.

I must have had that dream a hundred times when I was
a kid. Abraham Lincoln and I would be trying to escape
someone or something, and Lincoln would always desert
me, leaving me alone to face whatever monstrosity that
was chasing us. Funny thing was, whatever was chasing
us never showed up. I was just left there all by myself, all
alone, or maybe that was the monstrosity, being a little kid,
left all alone.

I never had to worry about being alone in real life,
though. I shared a room with other boys my age at a
foster home. It was either that or I stayed at a group
home. Group home is just a nice word for orphanage.

I wasn't an orphan, though. My mom just had some problems, and my dad — well I'd never met him. I was told he had been in a war and... that's all I really knew. One day in a group home library, I found a book about Disneyland. It sure looked like a lot of fun. Disneyland was in California, where it was always sunny and never snowed or rained. They had a bunch of fun rides there, and families would go and laugh and meet Mickey Mouse and eat ice cream. There was also an exhibit with a robot Abraham Lincoln. It walked around and recited the Gettysburg Address in a theater called The Hall of Presidents. The book said the robot was so lifelike that you couldn't even tell it was a robot. Wow! Disney sure looked like a lot of fun. Too bad I was never going to get to go. It was way too expensive. Hell, a lotta people didn't have enough money to take their own kids, let alone a bunch of foster kids. So I never got to go. I could only read about it, daydream, or draw pictures.

Don't worry, though. It all worked out in the end. I made it to California and to Disneyland. Sure, it wasn't until I was 27-years-old, half-crazy, and pretty much broke. But I made it.

Things weren't going very well where I was living. I had lost my job and gotten kicked out of my apartment. I got arrested for driving drunk, and then my girlfriend saw the writing on the wall and she broke up with me. Let's just say it wasn't the best week, and I guess something inside of me finally just snapped, because the only good idea I could come up with was to go to Disneyland and to assassinate the robot Abraham Lincoln. He'd been assassinated once when he was alive, so I was sure his robot doppelganger could use the same kind of hospitality. And, hell, this way I could go out in some kind of crazy blaze of fucked-up glory. Beats dying alone like some loser in a dead-end town. So the plan was to scrounge up enough money to get a Greyhound bus ticket to L.A. Then the only things I needed were an old snub-nosed revolver or maybe a sawed-off shotgun, some books, half a sheet of acid, and $79 to get into Disneyland. My further plan once I got into Disney was to give everyone in attendance at the Hall of Presidents communion (the acid) and then read'em some Alan Watts while it kicked in. Then I'd blow Lincoln's robot brains out when the fuzz busted in. I'd go down in a real, honest-to-goodness blaze of glory.

And it would have been great, too, had I not gotten lost. I guess that's what happens when you take acid in a strange metropolis and you ask hobos for directions. So somehow I ended up at a Zen monastery. I bullshitted the abbot into letting me stay for a few days, and a few days spread into a few months and into a few years. Everything was going pretty well, until one day, the feds rolled in and arrested the abbott and a few other monks. Turns out all that incense we were making? Well, it was some pretty good hashish. It was probably time to get moving on anyway. You can't

spend your whole life in a monastery. So I packed up and decided to go back home. Another monk and I raided the donation box and the gift shop till. I got enough for another bus ticket and maybe even enough to get a ticket to visit old robot Lincoln and Disneyland before I left. It would have been a shame to come all this way and not at least say hello. So that's what I did. I rode the bus in my monk robes to Disneyland.

It was a funny feeling standing in Disneyland in front of that glass case. You see, old robot Lincoln was no longer doing his Gettysburg Address in the Hall of Presidents. No, now he was retired and was all stripped down, his naked robot inner workings on display in a glass case for all to see. I, too, was naked, naked of all my anger and childhood issues.

I stood there in my orange robes chuckling softly to myself. I stood there so long that a guy came over and asked me if I was OK. I replied that I had never been calmer or clearer and that I was certainly glad I was able to do this without any anger or hatred.

I squeezed off the first round just a half-inch or so below Lincoln's left eye. The second bullet hit him square in the chin. Through the shattered glass, I saw his eye pop out and sparks fly from his beard. The screams were just as I'd imagined. The guard was on me now, and as he wrenched me to the ground, I saw Lincoln's beard catch fire and his head become engulfed in flames. I, too, was engulfed, engulfed in the peace and bliss that only a man who has truly achieved his destiny can feel. **OMMMMMMM...**

Good Seats

**I'm tired.
I spent most of the evening at
Spanky's adult emporium.**

I've got tickets to see Celine Dion in concert, and I need
a sex toy that not only is visually obvious from a good
distance, but also has the right amount of heft and balance
to be thrown at a great velocity over 15 to 20 meters.

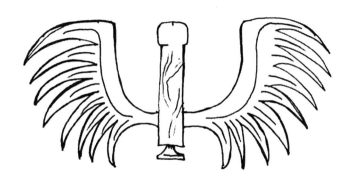

**"I spent all the money on cosmetic surgery for my dog.
It was worth it. She looks at least two to three years
younger."**

— Mahatma Gandhi

Murder Mystery

Today I saw a man sitting outside a Starbucks. He was just sitting there all by himself at a table, drinking a cup of coffee.

It struck me as odd. Something seemed amiss. I looked closer. Here was a 45 to 50-year-old white male in a polo shirt and jeans, just sitting at a table drinking coffee. He didn't look like he was doing anything other than the aforementioned drinking of the coffee. So I watched him closer. His lips weren't moving, and he didn't have an earpiece. I didn't even see a phone. I waited. He didn't seem to be fixated on anything in particular. There was a half-empty parking lot in front of him, then the road, and beyond that a wall. It was obvious he didn't have a laptop. He wasn't texting. He wasn't reading a book. He wasn't whittling a stick. He wasn't listening to his IPod. He wasn't even smoking a cigarette.

WHAT THE FUCK WAS HE DOING?!

I watched for a good 10 minutes, and the man did absolutely nothing but drink his coffee. Then, like a switch had been thrown, he finally got up and went over to the trash can. He put his cup in the can and walked to his car. He got in the car, started it up, and just drove off.
WTF?!

Little Debbie

I was surprised when I died.
God asked me a lot of questions.
He was like an excited little kid.
"What was it like to kiss a girl?!" He whispered.

You've never kissed a girl? I asked

"Naw." God blushed,
"For me there is no other."

"Fucking bullshit!" an angel piped up.

"Shut the fuck up, Todd!" God hissed.

Todd continued, "So that planet you destroyed
cuz that Debbie chick slapped you?"

"DEBORAH!" God roared. **"HER NAME WAS DEBORAH!
AND SHE DIDN'T SLAP ME. The whole thing was Steve's
fault anyway..."** he trailed off. Then he cleared his throat
and asked me if I'd ever been to an Applebee's.

Clueless

Somebody said something one time
and it was really beautiful.
Somebody said something one time
and it was really ugly.
Somebody said something one time
and it made you cry.

God spoke and the word became flesh.

What happened next, the pope
couldn't condone.

Someone said something one time
and your mother died.
Someone said something one time
and the parking meter ran outta money.

"Life is a boundless mystery,"
said a lizard, thoughtfully smoking a pipe.

Everyone knows
that you may already be a winner,
but I know
that you are already dead.
I went to the funeral
and everyone was being picked off

as if by a sniper,
one by one.
Of course, the authorities showed up,
but they never found
anyone.

Oh, sure, there were clues!
Tantalizing and delicious clues!

But the prime suspect turned out to be
an 8-year-old little girl.
Her alibi was an entire petting zoo
and several billion years of anticipation.

"If I had a blog... I'd write about kittens all day!!! =)"
— Satan

Hello, Dolly

I was being stalked by Carol Channing, she showed up at my office, my wedding, and even the muffler shop.

"Darling! You must come to the desert. We need you for the rocket launch!"

She had strong magic and began to alter my day-to-day waking reality. Everyone was turning into Carol Channing: my wife, my cat, Jesus and even my proctologist! It got so bad that even inanimate objects like the toilet would even start singing "Hello, Dolly" while I was trying to take a dump. And she was vulgar too, begging me to... well, I'll spare you the grisly details.

Finally, my mailman, Raoul, told me that he had an uncle who had a similar problem, only with Spanish-born entertainer Charo. He said that once his uncle traveled to Catemaco, Mexico, and brought back the spirit of a black dog, the problem stopped. So with nothing to lose, I immediately consulted Craigslist. I then went to the Humane Society and came back an hour later with a little black mutt named Chainsaw. I haven't seen Carol or heard a show tune since. But the funny thing is, now I kinda miss her.

Meanwhile, Down at Chuck E. Cheese's

Archaeologists made a significant discovery today in the southwest desserts of New Eurasia. The discovery is reportedly the largest of its kind and might hold great insights into the American way of life in the 20th Century A.D.

The site appears to be a large communal structure that contains the bodies of many children and several adult humans. What makes the discovery truly unique is that it also contains four large primitive robots, all dressed in animal furs. Scientists theorize the site was either a place of ritualistic sacrifice and worship or perhaps a large burial chamber.

"I pine for a simpler time. A time when a man could spend all afternoon in a tree, perfecting his Chewbacca roar, and not get arrested."

— Henry David Thoreau

Rush

So I'm at a urinal in the Applebee's restroom, standing next to some guy. Several seconds pass in awkward silence as I try to piss. I realize that the guy next to me isn't pissing either. I glance over at the guy, and I do a double-take. Its Rush Limbaugh. He looks over at me and nods in acknowledgment, and then it's all quiet a few more seconds before I start to pee. I realize Rush still isn't pissing, so I clear my throat and say:

"Hey, ya know Genghis Khan had a shy bladder."

"Is that right?" Rush snorts.

I continue, "Yeah, it was said that the only way he overcame it was by picturing himself urinating on the heads of his enemies."

"Hmmmph," Rush smiles.

I finish up and excitedly hurry back to tell my date, Elise, about my encounter.

Elise is this gorgeous black girl I met at an Obama organizing rally last week. She's maybe a little too left-wing and radical for me, but damn is she smart, and did I mention she's gorgeous?

Elise is whispering intensely to someone on her cell phone when I get back to our table so I order us two more Applebeetinis. Elise hangs up and immediately begins regaling me with some tale about her roommate, whom she has not seen in three days. Elise suddenly gasps in terror, her mouth agape and her eyes as wide as saucers. I hear a booming voice.

"Hey, thanks for the tip, piss buddy!"

It's Rush. He has a giant cigar in his mouth and is sweating profusely. He slaps me on the back and winks at Elise and whispers:

"Heya, sweetie!"

He ambles out the door with a couple of drunken MILFs, chortling the whole way.

Elise, still in shock, doesn't move. I chuckle and say, "Yeah, I uh… I just met Rush in the…"

"I should have known!" she blurts.

Her voice is trembling a bit. She begins to gather her things like she's leaving. "Hey, Elise," I say. "I… uh, I think you got the wrong, umm, uh, idea."

"Oh, I know what's going on here," she hisses. "You're a spy!"

"Oh, Elise," I roll my eyes. "Are you crazy? I don't know that guy."

She has all of her things in hand now, and she starts to leave. "Elise!" I half-yell.

She spins around and screams "FUCK OFF, PISS BOY!" The entire bar falls silent and stares at me as Elise stalks out.

The waiter shows up on cue with two bright-yellow Applebeetinis. "Thanks, man," I whisper.

I sit paralyzed, trying to act like nothing has happened. After what seems like an eternity, the bar noise and chatter start up again. I slowly look up. A toddler in a high chair is still staring at me. I casually avert its gaze by pretending to watch TV. Larry King is on. I lean back, close my eyes, and envision Larry happily patting his face in a golden stream of warm fluid.

Chihuahua

My dad had a tool chest full of elaborate metal devices.
He used them to fix dishwashers, furnaces, and refrigerators
out in the dark suburban tropics of medieval ranch homes.
One time on a job, he was in the basement of an old
house fixing the furnace. The homeowners'
Chihuahua was quite insistent in its belief
that my father had no rightly business in
the basement and proceeded to give
him holy hell. Dad tried to nicely
shoo it away with a pipe wrench
and "accidentally" caught the
poor pup right between the eyes,
killing it instantly. Luckily, the
dog was small enough to fit into
the bottom of Dad's tool chest.

Whenever Dad would tell this story,
he would be laughing so hard he
could hardly finish. Sometimes
I would have to finish for him.
"Boy, I betcha they still wonder
whatever happened to
that dog." Dad would be
laughing so hard he could
hardly breathe.

Lee "Fuckin" Marvin

When I was in the first grade, Billy Jensen brought Lee "Fuckin" Marvin to show-and-tell. I didn't know what the big deal was. Lee "Fuckin" Marvin appeared to be just some old man who smelled like gasoline. He was kinda funny though in that he kept trying to bum smokes off of our class hamster, Joe.

Billy sure was excited, about Lee "Fuckin" Marvin, maybe because he didn't have a real dad. Billy went on and on about how tough Marvin was and how he was a big movie star and a war hero. Marvin just curled up next to the hamster cage and fell asleep. Poor Billy.

Everyone forgot all about Lee "Fuckin" Marvin once it was Chris Willis's turn for show-and-tell. Chris Willis had an actual *Star Wars* X-wing fighter. Holy shit! A real X-wing fighter! Not some junk made out of Legos or cardboard, this was the real thing! You could put a Luke Skywalker action figure right in the cockpit, push a button and the wings popped open! Push another button and it made laser sounds, waking Lee "Fuckin" Marvin with such a fright, that he shot our hamster, Joe, with a pistol he had hidden in his sock.

Dissolving Problems With LSD

Backstage at some rave party/event, I was contemplating how to keep all the beer cold. We had several cases but only one cooler.

After struggling with this problem awhile, I realized there was no judgment or hierarchy and that all of us were all just this one awareness, experiencing itself in endless ways and plays of being.

I laughed & cried for a good 15 to 20 minutes.

I never did figure out how to keep all of that beer cold.

"Having children is not a big deal. The true dilemma... is in deciding what kind of wine to serve them with."
— Ayn Rand

$3.35 per Hour

I was a dishwasher at a Bonanza steakhouse when I was in high school. It was a terrible job.

One of the busboys was an elderly Jamaican gentleman named Clyde. I didn't understand most of what Clyde said, maybe a word or two. *Lobster, muthafucka,* and *bitch-ass* were some favorites. He smoked these giant joints, was always singing, and had this infectious wheezing laughter.

One night when we were closing up, some of the guys who were a little older than I tried to get Clyde to buy them some beer. Clyde sold them a wine bottle full of something homemade; it was clear and smelled like floor cleaner.

I sat out back with Clyde, and we watched 'em drink it. It was a warm summer night. One of the guys had pulled his Monte Carlo around and had the stereo going. "I Heard A Rumor" by Bananarama was playing. The guys were getting pretty wild, and I was getting a little nervous. My father was a pretty vicious drunk. Suddenly one of them turned into a bubble and began to float off. Then one by one, they all turned into bubbles and floated up and away. That Righteous Brothers song, "I've Had The Time of My Life," was playing now, and Clyde just laughed his Muttley laugh and walked back inside the restaurant. All was silent except for the music. When I turned around, there was a small boy standing there. He was so black he was blue. He looked almost like a little alien king of some kind. He had on a bunch of fancy gold jewelry. He smiled at me and cocked his head. He held out his hands and presented me with a golden fish. For some reason, I just started crying.

"Last night at McDonald's, I got a six-piece chicken McNuggets. Inside there were seven chicken McNuggets. I felt like I'd just high-fived a tiger."
— Tom Laundry

Master

I found my guru in a cheap roadside attraction.
An animatronic gorilla dressed as a magician.
He was sawing a woman in half.

Every so often, a child would appear
and put in a quarter.

The screams and hideous laughter...
I meditated in his presence for several years.

The attraction closed
and I was put in a hospital for the insane.
Now I sit in a big room all day with the others.

Every so often, a man comes in
and turns on the television set.

The screams and hideous laughter...

I fall to the floor, prostrate.
Master!

Walter Cronkite Upon Receiving the Global Governance Award at the UN in 1999

"So I go to this big mega-church every Sunday. I stay up drinking all Saturday night, which ensures that I'll have a really super, kick-ass, fun time."

"One particular Sunday, I walk into the bathroom after the service, and there are, like, five guys standing at six urinals. So I immediately walk into a stall, because I have a shy bladder. And I know all these guys at the urinals are all making fun of me — high-fiving, six-gun-shooting and tiptoe-dancing... cuz I can't PEE with the big boys, right?! So I'm feeling stupid, but then I come up with this great idea right on the spot. I pretend to snort drugs while I'm in the stall! And suddenly its dead silent, cuz now I'm the cool one, right?! And they are all just a bunch of squares."

Mutha Nature

My bubble pipe caresses
While my lover undresses
The whole world hungry
Mother Nature is in heat.

That fat, wild bitch
I've seen her destroy Winnebago's
With a flick of a wrist.
I've seen her make love to an
Entire forest.
Flowers and animals — a venerable orgy —
Swallowing entire sleepy villages whole,
But she knows little of human love
And even less about economic theory.

Sometimes, when no one's watching,
I find myself cheering her on
As she devours a trailer park or an outlet mall
"OH, OH! Get the big steeple!" I squeal.
"The one with all the stained glass and the golden cross!"

Ouroboros

Not many people know that Michelangelo's first version of the Sistine Chapel was just one big God orgy. Hot God-on-God action. And it was pretty hot. But then the pope and the cardinals all got involved and turned it into the middle-school make-out party we see today.

God can't just live out in the wide-open, and the Devil wasn't making any money, so the hide-and-seek began. Shame, Guilt, and other Milton Bradley games came into being. This is how Ouroboros, the tail-eater, became the tail-dragger, covering up its own tracks. And hell, we needed something to do until the internets was born.

One-Minute Music Review

Saying one has a favorite Bee Gees song is akin to saying that one has a favorite way of being kicked in the crotch. That said, "Emotion" by the Bee Gees is like being kicked in the crotch by a goddess. Might I add that she is wearing giant velvet bunny slippers and she's got that pouty, mean, Bettie Page look on her face. A sweet slow-motion disaster.

Fort Lauderdale, Florida, Friday May 28

There are women here who've had so much plastic surgery they look like aliens. Its kinda tempting.

I realized this while I was looking around, waiting in line for a full-body x-ray at the airport. For those who don't know, the full- body scanner gives a very accurate portrait of a person sans clothes, especially of a man's privates. So I, along with every other man in line, was trying to "chub" up a bit. I noticed some men openingly leering at a scantily dressed Puerto Rican girl, but most just had their eyes closed, fantasizing about God knows what. I joked with the guy next to me that they should have a fluffer. I didn't realize until I saw his collar that he was a priest. And yeah, maybe I took the joke a little far when I started pointing out little kids for him.

In Search of Chocolate Thunder

A couple of months ago down at Applebee's, we had a little birthday get-together for my dad. I got him a Darryl Dawkins throwback jersey. It was fitting not only because it was my dad's 53rd birthday and Dawkins' number was 53, but also because my dad had gotten me a Dawkins jersey and basketball when I was a little kid. I'll never forget that birthday. Dad and Mom where already separated, but he had come over for my birthday party. Years later, I found out he had been cheating on Mom and that he had spent a lot of money on some young secretary. Needless to say, Mom didn't want him around, let alone in the house, but she knew it was important to me so she relented and had him come over for my birthday. I didn't know anything other than Dad was home. I think I sat on his lap all day. We even got to watch a 76ers game on TV, one that Dawkins, my dad's favorite player, played in.

> **NOTE:** Dawkins, AKA "Chocolate Thunder," was a 6'11" basketball player from the '70s and '80s who was famous for slam-dunking the ball so hard that he would sometimes shatter the glass in the backboard. He was also famous for his unusual behavior and interesting sayings.

Also, another reason I won't forget that birthday was because my mom nearly burned down the house baking my birthday cake. I remember sitting across the street watching all the firemen run in and out of our smoky little house. My mom and dad were screaming at each other. I was mad too — all this craziness and no cake? It was horrible! Well, Dad never came by the house again, and as life went on, I learned there is a lot of pain and confusion in this old world but not nearly enough cake.

So back to Applebee's and my dad's birthday party. We had watched some basketball, eaten some nachos, and were finishing up some cake. Dad was sitting there eating his cake in his new throwback Dawkins jersey when he bit into something. It turned out to be a little, round piece of glass. He was OK, and he joked to me that maybe it was a piece of glass from a Darryl Dawkins shattered backboard. We all laughed. Then my aunt said, "You noticed the name of the dessert, right? Chocolate Thunder!"

They all laughed even harder, but my head swam a little. Dad looked at me like he just remembered something, and I had the most intense déja vù experience.

Three days later, I got a phone call. Dad had died in a car accident. I saw his face smiling at me. My head swam again. Only this time it seemed like it just kept on swimming. The funeral was a blur. I found out Dad had been thrown through the windshield, and all I could see was Darryl Dawkins shattering glass backboards. It's funny when someone dies — everyone feels bad and is real nice to you for a few days, and then life goes on like normal. Everybody just goes back to work. Well, I kinda... well, everything was still swimming for me, ya know. I stopped talking. I just couldn't make sense of anything. My girlfriend got really worried. My job was calling, wondering if I was coming back to work. So I just left, left everything. I threw my keys away, threw away my wallet, and left. I didn't need it. I don't need anything.

Then today, while at the library writing this, I was flipping through some old *Sports Illustrated* issues when I came across an article about Darryl Dawkins. The article said Dawkins at one point had taken a vow of silence, of which he later stated, "Nothing means nothing, but it isn't really nothing, because nothing is something that isn't."

I think maybe it's about time I go and pay Mr. Dawkins a visit.

"My retirement plan involves a safety deposit box and two sheets of acid."

— William Howard Taft

"Wrestling Midgets Killed by Fake Hookers"
– AP Headline, Mexico City, Mexico

A poem inspired by a true-life tragedy:

Alone
my heart shall wander
Inconsolable
through the streets of Tijuana
Devastated.

The locals will call out to me
"Hey, stoner dude!"
but I will not hear them.

For tonight there is an empty time slot on TLC,
a void that sings of sadness and mystery
and of all the loss you will witness
and of all the internet porn you will see
I kneel and pray to St. Rowdy Roddy Piper
that these "fake hookers" shall never get to thee.

My Dearest Sugar Muffin,

I had the bestest Valentine's Day ever mapped out. First, I was planning to go down to Ace Hardware, get possessed by the Devil, and eat a dozen red roses. Then, I was going to make your favorite goulash and serenade you with Black Sabbath's "Sabbra Cadabra" in six different octaves — my ass singing the lowest two registers whilst showering you with rose petals — but of course I got buried in paperwork, stress and all sorts of dumb bullshit down at the office. Next year, I promise I will throw Cleveland or maybe Cincinnati into the sun for you. Until then, please except this note and this 15 percent off coupon at participating Red Lobsters as a small token of my undying love for you.

You are awesome! I look forward to making tea for you during the next century while we watch Western civilization collapse into a shit pile run by fashion-conscious wiener dogs.

Love, yer old monkey, Beelzebub.

Hypnosis Reveals the Truth

I was particularly excited about that week's episode of **CHIPS**. According to the *TV Guide*, Ponch and John were going to bust up a ring of **car strippers!**

My 10-year-old mind fantasized about **Daisy Duke wrigglin' outta her tight lil' clothes, zooming up and down I-5 at 110 mph with Van Halen's "Running With the Devil" blasting off the 8-track.**

I didn't know that "car strippers" meant old white guys who steal rims.

I was truly devastated. And to tell the truth, it's all been downhill ever since.

SUNDAY, SUNDAY, SUNDAY!!!

Why is it that after watching football all day,
I have the strangest urge to take a fistful of Viagra
and copulate with a Dodge Hemi?

Rollins

We were headed out to the lake a few weeks ago, the song "Boys of Summer" came on the car radio. It wasn't the original Don Henley version. It was some new "pop punk" boy band cover. I would have changed the station or slipped in an Air Supply CD, but I was bound and gagged in the trunk. (Perhaps a story for another time.)

Anywho, the song dragged on until they got to the lyric "Out on the road today, I saw a Dead Head sticker on a Cadillac..."

Well, our smart-n-sassy vocalist had replaced the term "Dead Head" with "Black Flag." I have to admit I was a little surprised.

I spent the next several days contemplating what former Black Flag frontman Henry Rollins' reactions might have been upon hearing the song. I imagine they were something akin to the stages of grief, only with all the stages prenatally aborted, smashed, and replaced with vitriolic anger. Somewhere inside, though, I imagine old Hank had to be at least a little bit flattered. Perhaps later on, he was at an IHOP drinking coffee and writing. He got up, went to the bathroom, caught a glimpse of himself in the mirror, and blushed. Then he practiced mean, scary faces in the mirror until the assistant manager walked in on him.

Your
Ad
Here

I make commission selling ads. Every sale I make brings me one step closer to my dream of owning my very own giant, mechanical shark.

Health Care 2010

Patient: The new pills are awesome, but I just wish we could do something about the side effects.

Dr: What kind of side effects are you having?

Patient: Oh, the ushe… bleeding, projectile vomiting, anal depression, but the big problem now is that my left arm keeps falling off. I almost dropped a full tray of Whoppers on little Todd yesterday. Is there anything we can do about that?

Dr: Well, let's take a look at that arm.

(Patient hands Dr. left arm)

(Dr. makes interested doctor sounds)

Patient: Well, Doc, whattya think?

Dr: Yes, I've seen this before. Not sure what it is, but I think I have something that may work. *(hands patient a fistfull of packets)* **I got a bunch of these free samples at the drug reps' free luncheon yesterday. Here, take one of these three times a day every other day for eight days and then drink two gallons of this** *(places 5-gallon bucket on counter)* **before bed.**

Patient: What's it do?

Dr: Who fucking knows?! *(uproarious laughter)*
But the insurance covers it.

Patient: Yeah, but seriously, Doc?

Dr: Like I said, I'm not sure, but according to my secretary, you just lie in bed and watch the walls melt in a warm array of pastel colors. She said, "It was, like, really cool."

Patient: Sounds great!

Dr: Yeah. Well I gotta get. Say hey to the wife for me.

Patient: Doc, she died eight months ago on the operating table. Don't you remember? You were the attending surgeon.

Dr: Oh, yeah, the lawsuit. Now I remember. My insurance went up. Sooo… well, how are the kids?

Patient: Todd hasn't spoken since, and —

Dr: And that's why you went on the medication.
(snaps fingers) **Yep, it's all coming back to me now. Hmmm, yeah. Welp, I gotta run. See ya next week?**

Patient: You betcha, Doc.

Vacation

Much as the buffalo once did
now it's the Hyundais
that thickly cover these Black Hills.

The winds continually roar,
ordering half caf-half decaf
Grande vanilla soy
latte frappuccinos.

Ghost wanderer Crazy Horse
dances to more '80s hits
on the satellite radio.

And the lost pieces of yourself
flash bright red in a dark, dense jungle
so black and tangled
that sometimes
it's not even here.

A short story inspired by a picture of Elizabeth Taylor and Henry Kissinger embracing

I was raised by cruise ship attendants on a tropical island in the Caribbean. They would drop anchor a couple of times a week with fat Wisconsinites and feed me old buffet food. One day as I was finishing off a stale dessert tart, my father, chief purser Tad, told me he was not my real father. I was pretty upset, and I asked who my real parents were. Tad took one of the sacred picture books called TIME and tore a picture out of it. "Bingo," he said, "these are your true parents." And he gave me the picture mentioned above. I set out in search of them that evening.

I built a ramshackle raft out of old pop bottles and clamshell to-go boxes. I sailed around the islands, and I showed the picture to whomever I came across. Most people ran away from me or laughed. So I traveled farther and further.

One morning I came to a steep cliff. I somehow knew in my heart that the answers to all of my questions were at the top. It was a difficult climb. I broke my ankle and lost what few possessions I had left, but I held on tightly to the picture. When I finally reached the top a few days later, I saw a bunch of people sitting cross-legged in brightly colored bathrobes. They all ignored me, except for an old man named Leonard. Leonard took me to see an even older man. A man so old he looked like a turtle without its shell.

The older man was named Roshi. I liked him immediately. He told me that he knew my parents and that my mother's name was Elizabeth. She had magic purple eyes. My father's name was Henry; he was a great leader and had a funny voice like a robot machine. "They had both been hurt badly in their hearts by two different men," Roshi mused, "but the two men had one name, and the name was Dick." Leonard added that the picture I carried was taken by a famous artist named Andy. He went on to say that Andy took the picture at a large spiritual gathering called WrestleMania III. It was there, in a place called the Silverdome, that the forces of evil (Andre the Giant) were vanquished by Hulk Hogan in a steel cage match.

I was so happy to finally know the truth. I felt free. And though I loved the photo more than anything in the world, I gave it to Roshi. It was my only possession, and I wanted to give him something. I bowed down deep before him and held the picture up to him. He took it from my hands, chanted a few words I didn't know, and gently placed the picture on an altar. He clapped and I looked up and he smiled at me, a smile that still lives in my heart. A smile that reverberates and resonates to this day in ever-widening rings of grace. These feelings are especially strong whenever I see pictures or hear stories of Hulk Hogan.

Mordecai "Three Finger" Brown was a Hall of Fame pitcher who played for the Chicago Cubs back in the day. Legend was that Ol "Three Finger" lost two of his fingers in a fight with a dragon in the Middle Ages. When one of the fingers magically grew back, it was widely speculated that the hand was host to an evil spirit. It was with this possessed magic devil hand, that Three Finger, became a virtually unhittable pitcher. As a result, he threw 55,000 perfect games in his career.

Three Finger led the Cubs to a World Series title in 1907 and their last title in 1908. He retired from baseball in the 1920s to fish and sing, and in 1962 he moved to Saturn to live with his lover, Sun Ra.

"Dance like no one is watching. Sing like no one is listening. And I hope you enjoy being alone, because the only thing worse than your dancing is listening to you try to sing... Eh, sound like torture cat."
— Mother Teresa

Twilight VII

I peed my pants at the five-and-dime. I was buying a set of plastic vampire teeth, and the line was too long. So I came up with a brilliant idea. I just popped in the vampire teeth, and anyone who looked my way… SHOWTIME! They got the screeching vampire act and hopefully they didn't notice the pee pants.

Cartoon Mobster A: "Hey, Joe, did that 6-year-old vampire just piss himself?"

Cartoon Mobster B: "I dunno, Boss. I wuz too scared ta notice."

Later on, I used this trick (pulling focus) in my sales routine at the used car lot. Say, for instance, I did something embarrassing — like leave my zipper down or forget the customer's wife's name — I'd just shoot myself in the head. Worked like a charm. I tell ya, I sold a lot of Subarus in my day.

Cold Blooded

I had been in Italy for a couple of months. Nothing too glamorous, just working in a shipyard somewhere west of Venice.

Once I got back in the U.S., I found out that Ol' Dirty Bastard had died. I immediately phoned a friend.

Me: Dude! ODB died?!

F: Yeah... you didn't know?

Me: Dude, I was out of town! Why didn't you call me?

F: Oh, I dunno, I figured you woulda heard.

Me: Like some Italian is gonna run up to me in the street and say, "Scuse! Sir! Americano? I so sorry for you loss... the... Aged Dirty Bastard... he isa dead!!!?"

Hookers or Cake

You might wonder how this book got its name. *Hookers or Cake*, what does it mean?

There was an old picture that hung in the mayor's office. It was of Evel Knievel shaking hands with Richard Nixon. I always had a peculiar feeling about it, so one night after everyone went home, I took it down to the lab. I zoomed in 100 times on Evel's left eye and enhanced it. It was an address. I went to the address. It was a modest, 1970s-style, split-level ranch home in the suburbs. Inside, I found what appeared to be a dead parrot lying on a waterbed. I revived the parrot with some saltines and adrenaline. We became good friends. The parrot's name was Randy. One night a few years later while Randy and I played gin rummy, he sang me a song about a fire. The title of this book was never mentioned, but I sensed it, and Randy confirmed it by giving me "THE LOOK."

True Story

Surprise Party

I was at the liquor store filling up my cart for a surprise birthday party.

After fussing with 12-year-old bottles of this and that for a couple of lifetimes, I went to check out.

But there was no one.

There was no one but a half-open door. I snuck back behind the counter and peeked 'round the door. I was shocked to find a field of cherry blossoms and an old man wandering off in the distance. He wore a flowing kimono and jingly, jangly bells.

"HEY, ED!" I yelled after him.
"Wha... who the hell is minding the store?"

He turned, waved, and then turned back to wanderin' off over some hill.

I stood there for a bit. I could hear the birds chirping and smell the fresh spring breeze. Well, free booze, I thought. But when I turned back around to go into the store, there was nothing but endless rolling black space and a lot of stars.

"Surprise," said the cosmos.
"Surprise," echoed the voice in my head.

Reno

She was a kind of ancient snake charmer,
first seat clarinet in the high school band.

Squawks and honks
a form of blistering thunk.

Till we all forget about the ocean
quite completely.

I slow-danced with her once, to Prince's "Purple Rain" at a high school dance, and she smelled like strawberries and whiskey. She kissed me and forced her tongue into my mouth. I could feel her teeth — she had thousands of them. She told me to "put everything on the Steelers." I thought it was sexual innuendo, so I put my hands on her butt. What happened next I don't quite remember, but the papers declared that she'd destroyed more than half of Reno.

Home

One summer evening, leaving some fancy grocery store
in Portland, Oregon, a skinny old bum sidled up to me.
Funny thing was, he was trying to give me money. "Could
ya buy me a bottle of port?" he pleaded, holding out a
10-dollar bill. "They won't sell me none" he exhaled, his
shoulders slumping. He didn't seem that drunk, I thought,
they probably just didn't want him in the store. "Sure,
buddy," I shrugged. I had no place to be. So I went in and
got him the bottle he had described. Boy, was he tickled
pink when I came out and handed it to him. He even tried
to get me to keep the change. I gave him his money, but he
accepted only after I agreed to have a drink with him. Hell,
why not? I was just wandering around stoned, looking at
all the pretty colors, taking in the sounds and smells of the
city. If you've never been to Portland, it's a beautiful city,
especially when you're young and it's summer. I could
still smell the earlier rain in the air. I had a few bucks
in my pocket. Hmm, endless possibilities. The old bum
leaned against the concrete wall, spun the lid of the port,
and handed me the bottle. It tasted like sweet, rotten red
wine. We sat down right there on the sidewalk against
the storefront. We watched all the cars and people, and
he began to tell me stories. Tales of hopping freight trains,
picking fruit, a bar fight gone bad, someone dying, jail,
love, and leaving. He'd stop every so often, take a tug off
the bottle, and sum it all up in a sentence or two: "The man

who say he don't know fear is a lie." I would just nod, pass him a smoke, and listen.

Then he told me about the time that Mount St. Helens blew up. "We was all sacked out down on Third Street by the fountain. It was the middle of the afternoon, I woke up and it was dark, like it was nighttime, only it was daytime and it was snowing, snowing ash." He leaned in close to me, and his eyes got really big like a child's. He whispered, "We thought it was the end of the world!" Then he shook his head and smiled a big ol' toothless grin.

The President Just Emailed Me, Asking for $15

WTF, dude?!! I gave you $50 last year. Remember? A bunch of us chipped in so you could get a job. You got the job, right?!

Middle Management

Oh, gorgeous retard.
Oh, lover of high fructose corn syrup,
will you ever come to your senses?

You may already be a winner,
but only if you act now!

Jesus came back to earth 43 years ago,
but he got sucked into various pyramid schemes
and insurance scams.

They didn't crucify him with nails;
they did it with compounding interest.

Always the eternal optimist,
Jesus just kept working his office job
and making minimum payments.
He just knew he could make it up at the track.

The problem was... Jesus? He had terrible luck,
yet he never seemed to mind
as long as there was ice cream in the freezer
life wasn't half-bad.

*How come the people
in beer commercials
are never drunk?*
— Bodhidharma

1:48 p.m. Tuesday, Abdullah the Butcher's House of Ribs, Atlanta, GA

NOTE: Abdullah the Butcher is a 400lb hardcore professional wrestler, who goes by the moniker, "The Mad Man from Sudan," even though he's from Canada and his name is Larry. Abdullah is famous for his wrestling matches ending in bloodshed, as he always attacks his opponents with a foreign object, usually a fork or a piece of glass. Mostly retired these days, he lives in Atlanta, owning two restaurants, one in Atlanta and also one in Japan.

It was tucked into an outta the way place in a neighborhood that still had some character. The strip malls had yet to attack.

Unfortunately, the Butcher was not in. Nor did they sell T-shirts. "Sometimes we do, sometimes we don't," explained the cashier. "It all depends on the Butcher." What struck me was that this was a rib joint first and foremost. They had nothing to sell other than food. It was downright un-American.

I ordered the rib plate. It consisted of three bones plus two sides. I chose candied yams and mac-n-cheese. Cornbread and iced tea filled out the rest of my order. You should know that in the South, all iced tea is sweet tea, and it's delicious.

I wandered around the restaurant trying to look as inconspicuous as a tourist can. I looked at all of the old rasslin' pics that adorned the walls while I waited. It's a strange experience to look at pictures of half-naked men — covered in blood, wrestling, screaming — and to then eat a plate of barbecue sauce-covered ribs.

The food came out hot and all wrapped up in Styrofoam. I sat down at one of the tables and dug right in with my plastic weaponry. It was really good. Everything was homemade, the candied yams and cornbread where topnotch. There was a steady stream of people ordering take-out, a few construction workers dining in. I was the only white person, so my sense of being a silly tourist was compounded. Some of the old-timers were sitting around a small TV set watching some people's court show and carrying on.

All in all, it was a good visit, and I'm glad I stopped in. My expectations were a bit skewed, though. Abdullah the Butcher's House of Ribs isn't some kitschy over-the-top side show. No, it felt more like going to a quiet church and communing with everyday life. Eating food with the working man and the families, all while the Butcher earned a living too, whether it be carving up man or beast.

When I was older, I was a giant.
I would rise in the west like a siren,
shake the candy from my broken heart,
and attack sleepy miniature villages.

Eating office buildings like stacks of waffles,
dousing them with crude-oil syrup,
tearing open water towers to slake my thirst,
squeezing city buses like tubes of cookie dough.

My reign of terror lasted
until there was nothing left to smash,
and then it was nap time.

A Happy Mistake

My mom had let me stay up late to watch *The Tonight Show*
starring Johnny Carson. She told me that one of the most
brilliant minds in the world was going to be on and she
wanted me to see him.

I watched very intently.

Years later, in a deep meditative state, I realized that
she had mixed up Nelson Rockefeller with Charles
Nelson Reilly.

Easy

I didn't realize I was an asshole until I got a real job, got a car payment, got married, bought a house, and had a kid. Before all of that, I always thought I was a nice and easy-going guy. Come to find out I just had a nice and easy-going life.

Afterlife

My mom, Judy, passed away from cancer a few months ago. She had been ill for a couple of years. I was glad to be able to spend some time with her before she died. I was with her at hospice in the last few days. Me and my mom were never that close, but all these memories came flooding back. Birthday parties, holidays, her taking care of me when I was sick. Now I was the one taking care of her. Thankfully, she didn't seem to be in too much pain. She was so skinny and fragile… she looked like a little, helpless child. I remember the day she died. She just smiled and whispered, "I'm not going anywhere…" And then she passed.

The next week or two was a blur of dealing with her estate and consoling family and friends. I didn't think much about what she had said to me until one day, when I swore I heard her say my name in a crowd. Later that same evening, I found an email from her in my spam folder. It was dated five days after her death. It seemed that she was in Liberia and she had come across a great deal of money, but she needed me to send her money? I told her that she wasn't making any sense. I asked her what it was like to die. She didn't reply. And then just a couple of weeks ago, I got another email. Mom was talking all dirty about me satisfying women and making my cock bigger. I didn't know what to say. So I just wrote that I loved her and I haven't heard a peep out of her since.

It sure sounds like the afterlife is a wild and interesting time.

Free Wireless

Acceptance and peace bloom
in this crazy-ass wedding.

Jesus puts down the bong,
turns the bottles of water into boxes of wine.

My lion-tamer love lies down
with the robot that built Cincinnati.

Wires and tendons intertwine and
become wireless.
"ALL IS WIRELESS!" declares
the *New York Times*...

as we steal one another's bandwidth...
your black-heart router
blinking and nodding deep into the night.

Opening Act

About 15 years ago, I saw this band open for Blue Öyster Cult at the North Dakota State Fair. I don't remember their name, and sadly Blue Oyster Cult never got to go onstage because of the ensuing chaos.

I distinctly remember a middle-aged lady walking out onstage by herself. She was naked, painted white from head to toe and wearing a flaming clown wig. Bending over backward onto all fours, she began to twinkle. Then she grew and grew until she was the sky itself. It was then that the band members flew down out of her, upon raging steeds of thunder. I looked around at the crowd. They were just nodding and smoking cigarettes, like it was no big deal.

Then the band started to play. The sound seemed to come from everyone's eyes. Everything began to wobble and buzz. There was a lot of fire. People were screaming, laughing. Some just sat on the ground, rocking back and forth.

I don't recall much after that. The next thing I do remember is being arrested on the Canadian border. I was covered in blood and listening to Dan tell dirty knock-knock jokes. Dan was the ghost of the great Elk spirit. He had some fancy Native American name I could never remember, so we always just called him Dan.

So my children's book got rejected... AGAIN!

It's a simple, heart-touching story about a young boy whose entire family dies and he is shipped off to a foster family on a farm. Due to extreme loneliness, the boy begins to talk to and befriend the farm animals. Then one day, after seeing all of his farm animal friends slaughtered, he runs away to a old, abandoned house. There he tries to tame a family of wild opossums. The opossums attack him because they are wild, rabid animals. Over the next few hundred pages, the boy slowly dies of rabies while hallucinating he is the savior of humanity.

*I call it **Mr. Giggles Finds a Home.***

Love Her Madly

**More evidence was uncovered last week
hinting that Jim Morrison is still alive.
The following was discovered in a
Barnes & Noble in Emporia, Kansas.**

I awoke this morning
To the sounds of Paris burning.
When I looked out the window,
All I saw was you,
Which in this case
Was a motel Super 8 in Witchita.

Later, I ate a ham sandwich
That I found on the sidewalk.
It was moldy and terrible,
But my love ate it,
Because it was YOU.

I passed out shortly thereafter.
When I awoke, you were a pony,
And we made love.
The pony was a vicious, mean lover,
And I am now covered with scars.
But I love that pony,
because that pony is YOU.

I died in '70, '75, '82,
Each time resuscitated by the lizard men.
I am their immortal king.
They say I know what to do.

But I don't know anything
But this sweet, wild love
That I have for everything,
Because everything is you.

You think you can escape me,
But my love will devour your shoes.
You think you can run barefoot, laughing,
But I am the gum that you step in,
The horse manure too.

Our love is not easy,
Maybe it's because you are a crazy bitch
Who copulates with trees — I dunno.
All I know is that my love is hungry.
Baby, please! Turn into some tacos.

Death Belongs To...

I held you close
like a bowl of warm chili.
In vain I treated your mortal wound,
Packed it with three cups
of really good butterscotch pudding.
I ate the fourth.
It was sweet.

Actually, it was technically the third cup,
cuz I got hungry halfway through the second.

And really, if we're being, like, totally honest?
I ate like half of the fourth cup too
cuz your mortal wound was full...

Full of really good butterscotch pudding.

Where were we?
Oh yes, your mortal wound.

**Yeah, you were all like,
"I'm dying and I love you and shit,"
and I was being all stoic**

cuz I thought maybe the whole thing might be a practical
joke and I didn't want to be crying like a bitch on television.

So I held you close, and I looked all tough
and cool into your eyes.

And you where like, "God, you're so fucking hot, Todd."
And I was like, "Ditto, baby."

And we kissed and the music swelled
and you began to fade.

I held you even closer as you whispered,

"I will always love… Michelob."

And you breathed your last, and I cried,
"It's what the weekends were made for, baby!"

The doctors later explained, the part of your brain that really
loves Michelob had set loose like a wildfire, as your various
physiological systems shut down.

You left this mortal coil in a death-induced Michelob frenzy.

And I for one think that's pretty damn classy. But then
again, you were and always will be one classy lady.

8:23 a.m. Tuesday, Miami International Airport

Made it to the airport in plenty of time, but I had a little trouble getting through security. It seems that a bottle of English Leather and a flask of Macallan 12-year-old Scotch that I had in my possession were a little over the three-ounce liquid limit. Thinking quickly and not daring to waste good Scotch, I just downed the Macallan and dosed myself thoroughly with the English Leather. Then, picking my cigarette back up off the table, I grinned at the nice security lady. "You gotta ashtray, hon?" I winked.

After the subsequent interview and strip-search, I found myself a little pressed for time. I had to sprint all the way to my gate, with shoelaces untied and my belt unbuckled. I imagined this is how John Kruk must've felt going from first to third on a single up the middle. I was getting lightheaded, dizzy, and out of breath. I needed air, but all I could smell was English Leather and Scotch. It was as if I was being suffocated by James Garner.

That was my first heart attack.

Perhaps, God is just a sentimental monster.

Hemingway

I finally read *The Sun Also Rises*. It was damn good. It wasn't until someone asked me what it was about that I realized how good it truly was. For instance, check out this passage:

"We had absinthe at the café; no one was drunk, so we had dinner. We ate lamb with a few bottles of wine and then 14 more bottles for dessert. Hal showed up, fresh from the states. He had just finished his book, so to celebrate, we soaked a cat in gin and ate it. Hal's wife, Judy, whom I've slept with, is also a writer. I slept with her book too, and it was lousy. The waiter came by and we dosed him with port and drank his blood. I was starting to feel a bit drunk, so I went outside for some air. I waxed poetically about how awesome Paris is for a paragraph. Then the blonde I'm in love with waved at me from across the street. I nodded, and she made her way toward me, fucking and drinking her way through the crowd. I had a few dozen whiskeys while I waited."

That's the whole book. A bunch of Americans drinking their way through Paris and Spain, passing around a drunk blonde, and waxing poetic about the scenery. But that's Hemingway, he could make eating a bowl of Cap'n Crunch sound epic.

In the future,
when I'm a young girl,
fighting giant, alien spiders,
on a distant and far-a-way planet...

This is the picture that I will keep in my locket.

I will take it out and gaze upon it,
when I am battle weary and forlorn
as I find that it refreshes my very soul.

Mr. Chief Billy

Who's the Boss was playing on the TV. I wasn't really paying much attention. It was the episode where Tony and Angela have a couple of drinks and end up kissing each other. They're laughing, running around the kitchen throwing flour, and chasing each other. Suddenly, they end up in each other's arms and they passionately kiss. The studio audience goes wild, and I shake my head and go back to something I'm reading on my laptop.

I glance up from my laptop because the TV has gone totally silent. I see Tony and Angela both looking directly into the camera as it zooms in tight on their faces. They begin to chant something repetitive that I don't quite understand, and then it becomes clearer.

"Mr. Chief Billy, Mr. Chief Billy, Mr. Chief Billy…"

The TV screen flickers, and I see an old black-and-white image of an old man with a mustache. I stare at it closely as it seems to be moving slightly. Like someone has paused the tape and is forwarding it one frame at a time. I glance around the room, and when I look back, I notice that his eyes are becoming large and soft, almost like a gentle, sad monster of sorts. The man smiles and says lovingly, "My dear, everyone cares… but nobody knows." And it's strange because I am overwhelmed with these feelings of peace and joy. I almost feel as if this man is God or something. Then part of the man's mustache begins to vibrate and move. It morphs into a large, colorful butterfly that seems to flutter right out of the TV screen. Slowly, the butterfly flickers and floats toward me, turning into a kind of rainbow-colored liquid that then swims into my mouth. I don't panic because the whole time I feel as if I am being filled with this warm, healing light. It's like I am being filled with love. I blink, and now I'm inside of the TV looking out, looking out at all the families who are gathered in their various living rooms watching TV. I am looking out at all the little kids, moms, dads, and elderly couples. I feel such intense love for them all now. I see the old man again and now he's sitting in a room all alone. He's looking at me, and his face begins to decompose as he whispers. "There is absolutely nothing to be afraid of, my dear." I blink my eyes again and I'm back sitting on my couch. The TV screen is silent and blank except for the message:

To be continued...

Follow Lewd Pony Press online at
WWW.LEWDPONYPRESS.COM
for future projects and bonus content.

LaVergne, TN USA
13 August 2010
193290LV00001B/2/P